dick bruna

KT-213-762

miffy's bicycle

SIMON AND SCHUSTER
London New York Sydney Toronto New Delhi

When I grow up, thought Miffy,

there's something I would like –

to take a trip, if I'm allowed,

touring on my bike.

I'll pedal through the meadows,

so colourful and bright.

I love to be near flowers.

They're such a lovely sight.

Past the pond I'll cycle

where white ducks wait for bread.

I'll take some in my pocket

to make sure they get fed.

I'll ride right through the forest.

That's difficult to do,

because there are so many trees

to trace the trail through.

And then I'll pedal up the hill.

That part is steep and long.

But even so I'll manage it

for by then I'll be strong.

High on that hill there stands a house

so small and white and neat,

the home of Auntie Alice

who is so kind and sweet.

Alice is my favourite Auntie,

oh, she's really great!

She bakes delicious cookies

like these ones on the plate!

But soon I'll have to ride back home

as time goes ticking past.

Watch me as I race downhill.

Aren't I going fast!

I think I should be careful though

as I could take a fall.

To have a nasty accident

just wouldn't do at all.

I'll make sure that won't happen

by never going too fast.

I'm riding through the forest now.

Wave as I go past!

Of course, it could start raining.

And then I'd get wet through.

But riding through a rain shower

can be exciting too!

When I get back home again

I'll give my bike a clean.

I'll wipe it till it's once again

a shining bright machine!

But all that will be later on

when I'm a bigger bun.

I hope I'll grow up quickly

for cycling will be fun.

original title: nijntje op de fiets
Original text Dick Bruna © copyright Mercis Publishing bv, 1982
Illustrations Dick Bruna © copyright Mercis bv, 1982
This edition published in Great Britain in 2014 by Simon and Schuster UK Limited,
1st Floor, 222 Gray's Inn Road, London WC1X 8HB
Publication licensed by Mercis Publishing bv, Amsterdam
English translation by Tony Mitton, 2014
ISBN 978-1-4711-2281-1
Printed and bound in China
All rights reserved, including the right of reproduction in whole or in part in any form
A CIP catalogue record for this book is available from the British Library upon request
10 9 8 7 6 5 4

www.simonandschuster.co.uk